MONSTER MACHINES

ARCTIC ICEBREAKER

LOUIS S. ST-LAURENT

John Bankston

2001 SW 31st Avenue
Hallandale, FL 33009
www.mitchelllane.com

First Edition, 2020.

Author: John Bankston
Designer: Ed Morgan
Editor: Lisa Petrillo

Little Mitchie is an imprint of Mitchell Lane Publishers.

Names/credits:
Title: Arctic Icebreaker Louis S. St-Laurent / by John Bankston
Description: Hallandale, FL :
Mitchell Lane Publishers, [2020]

Series: Monster Machines
Library bound ISBN: 9781680204520
eBook ISBN: 9781680204537

Photo credits: Freepik.com, Shutterstock, Getty Images, p. 9 Aleksandr Mariy van Maanen, p. 10 NOAA public domain, p. 13 NOAA public domain, p. 14 Patrick Kelley, U.S. Coast Guard, U.S. Geological Survey, p. 18 NOAA public domain

Contents

Chapter 1

Saved!

The two men were stranded. They had been hunting. On the way home, their small, open boat hit a rock. It sunk.

The water was freezing. They climbed onto the rock. Their sliver of safety was quickly disappearing.

Frozen waters present danger off the coast of Canada.

In the world's coldest places, help is hard to find. Ice can sink ships when they get stuck in frozen rivers. Planes and helicopters have trouble flying in frigid weather when wings and **propellers** freeze over.

The men's boat went down in Canada's Gulf of St. Lawrence, off the coast of Newfoundland. "It was a windy, snowy night," **winch** operator Kirby Vatcher told writer Peter Lourie. Vatcher was onboard the Canadian Coast Guard Ship (CCGS) Louis S. St-Laurent when the call came in. The ship is an icebreaker. It is specially equipped so it can travel to places few other boats can reach.

Canadian Coast Guard Ship (CCGS) Louis S. St-Laurent is strong enough to clear icy harbors.

"We were on anchor in Cow Head, [Newfoundland]," he remembered. "We had to jump onboard a fast rescue craft. We had to get them off that rock before the tide carried them away."

Vatcher succeeded. The men were saved.

The Louis St-Laurent Icebreaker doesn't just rescue people. It clears icy harbors blocked by giant floating ice chunks. It supplies coastal villages. It is even helping us learn why oceans are growing warmer by using its scientific monitoring equipment. Although it uses modern technology, icebreakers were first designed hundreds of years ago.

On August 22, 1994, the Louis S. St-Laurent and the U.S. Coast Guard Cutter Polar Sea became the first North American ships to reach the North Pole.

Chapter 2

A Better Boat

Imagine being on a boat in winter. The rough sea is filled with sheets of ice. These **floes** can be miles long. As the boat passes, the floes squeeze against its sides. The boat is held fast. There is no escape.

A Russian koch was an early icebreaker.

One thousand years ago, Russian boat builders settled along the White Sea. The sea was named for the white-colored ice blooming along its surface. They built a special kind of boat. Called a "koch," it was one of the first icebreakers.

Like other wooden ships, the special icebreaking koch was powered by wind. One or two **masts** held sails. These were attached to the hull or body of the ship. Extra planks were nailed around the **hull** like a belt. Below it, the **keel** could be removed. Then the boat could be carried across the thickest ice.

Icebreaker ships have improved. They have three things in common. They have strong hulls. Instead of planks, iron bands are used. The bow or front end's shape guides ice chunks away from the hull. And all icebreakers use powerful engines to push through floes or break up sea ice.

In Canada, ice jams along the Saint Lawrence River can cause flooding along the river banks. The country also needs ships to **navigate**. The CCGS St-Laurent icebreaker can do both.

The Louis S. St-Laurent approaches the Coast Guard Cutter Healy in the Arctic Ocean.

Named for the country's 12th Prime Minister, the ship is nearly 400 feet long and weighs more than 30 million pounds. Built by Canadian Vickers Ltd., it cost more than 80 million Canadian dollars. Crews piloting the ship began icebreaking and conducting research onboard in 1969. Today it is the largest ship in the Canadian Coast Guard fleet.

FAST FACT

The CCGS S. St-Laurent was built to last just thirty years, but it keeps getting improved so it can keep going. Its hull has been lengthened. Its engines are more powerful. In January 2017, more than $14 million was spent to keep the ship working.

Chapter 3

Changing World

The Arctic Circle sits atop the planet. Once a year, the Sun never sets. Six months later, it doesn't rise. Thousands of people live in Canada's far north. During harsh winters there, they are cut off from the rest of the world reaching them. The CCGS St-Laurent helps to make their lives easier. Icebreakers do more than help other ships navigate or clear icy harbors. They bring food and medicine to Arctic villages.

For people in the remote towns, it can be hard to predict when supplies will arrive. Bad weather slows even icebreakers. When other boats lose power, icebreakers tow them. Needed supplies can be delayed for weeks. Villagers are glad when they spot the bright red and white colors of the Canadian Coast Guard's ships.

Icebreakers can saves lives in the far northern places on Earth.

Onboard the CCGS St-Laurent, a crew of 55 is ready to help. Most grew up in Newfoundland or Labrador on the eastern-most tip of Canada, places with brutally cold winters. Yet they are shocked by recent changes. The Arctic is getting warmer. Year-round ice is suddenly melting.

The St. Laurent cuts a one lane highway north thorough the ice.

When solid ice melts, it leaves behind chunks. These chunks can crash into boats. Sometimes ice re-freezes, stranding ships. Along the coast, melting ice means rising seas and floods reaching deeper past the riverbanks. The St. Laurent is being used to help scientists learn why the Arctic is growing warmer.

"Less ice means more icebreakers, more ice also means more icebreakers," Pierre Leblanc, former commander of the Arctic Canadian Forces explained in *The Maritime Executive* magazine.

FAST FACT

The CCGS S. St-Laurent can break through all three types of ice: first-year ice like that in the Gulf of Saint Lawrence that thaws and freezes during the year; harder multi-year ice that hasn't melted for many years; and the hardest type of ice—glacial ice.

Chapter 4

How to Break the Ice

Breaking the ice takes power. In the 1970s, the Louis S. St-Laurent Icebreaker used steam-powered boilers. These powered three electric motors. In the late 1980s, they were replaced with five diesel engines.

A diver checks out the propellers of the Louis S. St.-Laurent.

Those engines deliver a total of 30,000 horsepower to the three propellers. One horsepower is what's needed to move a vehicle one foot per second. Today cars generally have under 300 horsepower.

Usually the Louis S. St-Laurent only needs half its power. When the ship hits solid ice, it can slam through it with a burst of 25,000 horsepower.

The icebreaker uses its sharply pointed hull to help cut through ice dangerous to ships.

The ship carries two helicopters. These travel over land and sea to gather scientific measurements.

Icebreakers' **bows** are created to slide over ice and break it. That's one reason the CCGS St-Laurent does so well—it the heaviest of the CCGS's 17 icebreakers. The St-Laurent's sharp hull is called an "ice knife." It is protected by a two-inch thick steel "ice belt."

Besides its shape, small holes dot the front of the hull. Air from the ship is pushed through the holes, which helps the hull glide through ice. It lets the ship get through both solid ice and the chunks and sludge it creates.

FAST FACT

Arctic sailors face many types of ice with descriptive names. These include: baby-ice (new ice); black sheet ice that is so dark it looks like the water at night; calf ice that violently surfaces; and pancake-ice, round patches of sludge that makes the sea look paved.

Chapter 5

Power

The CCGS St-Laurent Icebreaker isn't known for speed. It is known for power. The famous British luxury cruise ship the Queen Mary, now retired, is seven times heavier, but both ships have the same heavy-duty steering gear. Along the Arctic Ocean, sea ice can be more than ten feet thick. But when fierce wind whips sheets of ice together, they grow bigger. The icebreaker has broken through ice ridges nearly 40 feet thick and almost 200 feet wide.

Traveling onboard is always an adventure. "It is quite a feeling to be in the middle of the Arctic Ocean," wrote teacher Émilie Hébert-Houle during a summer trek onboard the ship. She described how five hundred miles from shore, there is just ice and water and ship. "The ice changes—it gets thinner, thicker, blue, white, pressure rides higher, sharper, rounder. Then the ship makes its way to a puddle and follows a series of puddles before hitting ice again."

Despite a warming Arctic, there is still a need for the icebreaking St-Laurent.

FAST FACT

The first explorers of the Arctic seas were the indigenous people like the Inuit and Saami. They used kayaks which could not break the ice but were light enough to carry over it.

Map

map to the North Pole

Specs

Stern

400 feet

Bow

What You Should Know

- The CCGS Louis S. St-Laurent is the largest ship in the Canadian Coast Guard and one of the largest ice-breakers in the world.
- It is more than 50 years old and still in use.
- It uses five engines with a total of 30,000 horsepower.
- It weighs more than 30 million pounds.
- The ship is nearly 400 feet long and 80 feet high.
- The ship is named for the country's 12th Prime Minister, Louis St-Laurent, who helped the British colony Newfoundland become Canada's 10th province.
- During its historic 1994 trip to the North Pole, it crossed through nearly 3,000 miles of Arctic Ice. Its first Arctic crossing took it from the Pacific to the Atlantic Ocean.

Glossary

bow The forward part of a boat

floes A large sheet of floating ice

glacial Thick, slow moving and mountainous ice

hull A ship's main body, especially the two sides, the bottom and the deck

keel A boat part connected to the hull on the bottom, that helps steady the boat from tipping over

masts Thick post for holding sails

navigate Direct a ship's route

propellers Blades that spin to help move a ship

winch A device for lifting that uses a chain wrapped around a drum to lower a rope

Find Out More

Aloian, Sam. *How a Ship is Built*. New York, NY : Gareth Stevens Publishing, 2016.

Adamson, Thomas K. *Ships*. Minneapolis, MN : Bellwether Media, Inc., 2017.

Richardson, Gillian. *Ten Ships That Rocked the World.* New York: Annick Press. 2015.

Graham, Ian. *Fifty Ships that Changed the Course of History: a Nautical History of the World.* Richmond Hill, Ontario: Firefly Books. 2016.

On the Internet

Basic facts about an Icebreaker Ship
https://www.icebreaker.fi/basic-facts-about-icebreaker-ships/

See what this mighty icebreaker looks like, and how it does its job
"CCGS Louis S. St-Laurent - Canadian Coast Guard,"
http://www.ccg-gcc.gc.ca/folios/00019/docs/Louis-StLaurent-eng.pdf

To learn the parts of a boat
http://www.schoolofsailing.net/terminology.html

Index

About the Author

Growing up in Vermont, I noticed how the rivers and streams near my house changed. Bone-dry in summer and frozen during the winter, they would swell with large chunks of ice during the first spring thaw. Listening to them slam into the shore line and each other, it's hard to realize there are crews on boats that bravely venture into these hazardous conditions. This is why learning about these icebreakers was so interesting. Today I live far from ice floes in Miami Beach, Florida—where I often complain when daytime temperatures dip below 80 degrees Fahrenheit.